I.D.

I.D.

Vicki Grant

orca soundings

Orca Book Publishers

Text copyright © 2007 Vicki Grant

Library and Archives Canada Cataloguing in Publication

Grant, Vicki
I.D. / written by Vicki Grant.

(Orca soundings)
978-1-55143-696-8 (bound) / 978-1-55143-694-4 (pbk.)

I. Title. II. Series.
PS8613.R367I2   2007 jC813'.6   C2006-907053-9

Summary: When Chris finds a wallet on the street, he is tempted to
take on someone else's identity.

First published in the United States, 2007
Library of Congress Control Number: 2006940598

Orca Book Publishers gratefully acknowledges the support for its
publishing programs provided by the following agencies: the Government
of Canada through the Book Publishing Industry Development Program
and the Canada Council for the Arts, and the Province of British Columbia
through the BC Arts Council and the Book Publishing Tax Credit.

Cover design by Doug McCaffry
Cover photography by Getty Images

Orca Book Publishers
PO Box 5626, Station B
Victoria, BC Canada
V8R 6S4

Orca Book Publishers
PO Box 468
Custer, WA USA
98240-0468

www.orcabook.com
Printed and bound in Canada.
Printed on 100% PCW recycled paper.
11 10 09 08 • 6 5 4 3

For Eliza, Edwina, Teddy and Ed
with love and awe.
V.G.

Chapter One

I shouldn't have stopped. I was late already. But if you see a wallet on the sidewalk, what do you do? You stop.

I picked it up. I looked around. I could only see one person, an old guy, walking his dog.

Mr. Oxner was going to kill me. I'd already been suspended a couple of times for not showing up, flunking out, mouthing off, whatever. He'd gone crazy at me the day before. He said this was my last chance. If I so much as chewed gum in class—that's what he said—I was out for good. Expelled.

Like I cared.

I wanted to say, "Shove it." I didn't need anyone—especially Oxner—telling me what I could or could not do.

But I needed a place to stay. I needed to eat. If I got expelled, my stepfather would totally lose it. He'd make me go back to working checkout at the grocery store for six bucks an hour. He'd probably try to kick me out of the house. He'd for sure make my life hell. (Like it wasn't already.)

I could just hear him going on and on about how I'd screwed up again. How I'd never amount to anything. How I was a waste, deadweight, a jerk.

Yeah, right. Takes one to know one. That's what I'd be thinking—but I wouldn't say it. I'd just have to keep my mouth shut.

I couldn't hack that. There's no way I could just stand there while Ron spat all over me and Mom cried and Mandy didn't. The kid was only fourteen but she couldn't even cry anymore. She'd seen it all before.

I had to get to school. I had to keep Oxner happy for another month. Then I'd graduate. I'd get a job—like a real job—and get out of the house for good.

I looked at my watch. I looked at the old guy. I could tell he wasn't rich. I didn't want his dog to go hungry. I figured I could make it.

I ran over to him. I went, "Hey!" I said it too loud. He put his fists up like he was going to hit me. It was pathetic. He must have been eighty.

"Did you lose a black wallet?" I said. He put his hands down and laughed.

He said, "Whoa, there, young fella! I thought I was going to have to show you what for! And I could have too. Don't let this gray hair fool you. I used to be a boxer, you know..."

I cut him off. I showed him the wallet. "This yours?"

"Could be," he said. "How much money's in it?"

I pulled it open and counted the bills. "About seventy-five bucks," I said.

"Nah," he said, "I wouldn't take it off your hands for anything less than a hundred!" He had a good laugh about that.

I could have smacked him. I didn't have time to waste on some old geezer and his stupid jokes.

I swore—and scared him again. I stuffed the wallet into my back pocket and ran.

I made it to math class just in time. I skidded into my desk right as the bell stopped ringing. Oxner couldn't say a thing.

I looked straight at him and laughed.

He put on this prissy smile and said, "So glad you could make it, Christopher." I could tell he was really pissed off he couldn't do anything to me. He started writing on the board like a maniac. The chalk snapped in half and he muttered something under his breath.

"What was that, sir?" I said. "Did you say something?"

He went all white and twitchy.

"Nothing," he said. "I didn't say anything." Yeah, right. Like we all didn't know he was swearing. Poor baby broke his chalk. What an idiot.

Alexa Doucette turned around and winked at me. She was laughing. She whispered, "Nice job! You so nailed him!" I liked that. I never knew she'd even noticed me before.

I had a pencil and some paper. I brought my textbook. If Oxner asked, I even knew what page we were on. Everything was going great. I was bulletproof. I smiled back at her.

It's funny now, but I remember sitting there thinking, "This just might be my lucky day."

Chapter Two

Nothing makes me happier than pissing Oxner off. I felt so good. I almost liked school. I didn't skip any classes. I didn't make any smartass remarks. I even managed to stay awake all through Modern European history. That was a first.

It didn't hurt that Alexa was in that class too. Concentrating on her was way easier than concentrating on some dead king or something.

After class, a bunch of guys said they were going to Joe's Big Slice for pizza. Alexa was going too. She said, "Are you coming, Christopher?"

It really burns me when Oxner calls me by my full name, but it didn't bother me at all when Alexa did it. I shrugged and said, "Sure, why not?"

It was a dumb question. If she thought about it, Alexa could probably have come up with lots of reasons why not. Like, for starters, my stepdad is a truck driver for her dad's construction company. She's rich. I'm not. She's smart. I'm not. She lives in this big fancy house. I don't.

Believe me, I don't.

But I wasn't thinking that then. I was thinking, Alexa Doucette is hot for me. I was all right with that. I wouldn't be skipping any classes for a while.

I never go to Joe's after school. I can't stand the frigging lineups. That day, I didn't mind them. Alexa was standing right beside me.

She hates Oxner too. "He's such a dork," she said.

13

I laughed.

She said, "What's so funny?"

I said, "I bet *dork* is the worst thing you've ever said about anybody."

Her neck got all red and blotchy. She looked away.

"It's true, isn't it?" I said and poked her with my elbow. She didn't say anything. I poked her again. She slapped my arm away and laughed, even though you could tell she was trying not to.

She said, "Well, what am I supposed to call him?"

"I could give you lots of suggestions," I said. I opened my mouth like I was going to let rip with a couple of good ones.

"Shhh," she went. "I don't want to hear them!" She was pretty cute.

"Okay," I said. "So tell me why you think he's a...dork then."

She really got into it. Her face went all serious.

"Remember that assignment he had us do on famous mathematicians? I did a lot of research on it. My mother's a professor and she checked it all for me. I thought I was going to do really well, but then Oxner went and took five points off just because I printed it on the wrong size paper. Five whole points! Just for that! It's going to totally blow my average."

"Gee," I said. "I wonder how many points he's going to take off my assignment for not turning it in at all?"

"You didn't turn it in?" she said. She was all shocked. Rich kids are so funny. She looked at me like I'd just told her I'd kidnapped an old lady or something. "How come?"

"Didn't get around to it."

She stood there just shaking her head at me until Joe asked what we wanted.

"Extra pepperoni and a Coke," I said.

"Vegetarian and a spring water," she said. I should have known.

"Is this together?" Joe said.

I said, "Yeah."

Alexa said, "No. No."

I put my hand up and said, "Yeah. How much is it?"

I should have found that out first. "Eight dollars and fifty-six cents—before the tip," Joe said, like he always does. The guy's got one joke.

I forgot he charges more for vegetarian. I had maybe six bucks and change in my jeans. I put it on the counter. I checked my jacket, both pockets. I found four cents. I was getting nervous. I don't like looking bad. Alexa was making these little noises like she was going to say something. Joe— Mr. Funny Guy—wasn't laughing anymore. He didn't like me holding up the line.

I didn't want to have to ask one of my buddies for some cash.

Then I remembered.

"Sorry," I said. "I forgot I put my money in my back pocket."

I took out the black wallet and handed Joe a ten. "Keep the change," I said.

Chapter Three

Alexa gave me her phone number. She didn't want to at first. She said her parents didn't like her giving out personal information to boys they didn't know.

"It's just in case I have a homework question," I said. I winked. She smiled and went all blotchy again.

"You wouldn't want me to get in trouble with The Dork again, would you?" I said. She sort of laughed at that. She tore a little piece out of her notebook and wrote the number down. I put it in the wallet. Something feels so great about slipping a girl's number in between a couple of twenties. It made me feel like I was the type of guy who'd have a car parked out front.

I hung around talking to Alexa until she had to go study. I missed my bus. It took me forty-five minutes to walk home. It was pouring by the time I got there. I was soaked.

You'd think I'd get some sympathy.

Right.

My mother went ballistic. I didn't even have a chance to get my jacket off and she was screaming at me.

"Where were you?" She slapped a pot down on the stove and spaghetti sauce splashed all over her store uniform. My sister took off upstairs.

Mom was screeching at me. "I told you! I told you fifty times you had a job interview today! My boss didn't want to stay late today, but he did. He's a busy man, but he stayed late because I put my job on the line and I begged him to. Why? Because I didn't want you to have to miss any more classes. I begged my boss to stay late in order to make things easier for *you*. Not me. *You.*

"Then you don't even show up! You don't even bother calling! How could you possibly miss your interview? How could you humiliate me like that? What's the matter with you? Are you lazy? Are you mean? Or are you just stupid?"

She stared at me as if she actually expected me to answer. I turned away so she couldn't read my lips and hung my jacket on the bannister.

"And don't leave your clothes all over the place!"

She ran over and threw the jacket on the floor.

I couldn't even pick it up. She was about six inches away and yapping at me like some little bulldog.

"I am so sick of you and your mess and your screw-you attitude! It's time you grew up. It's time you started paying your own way, contributing to this family. And I know the perfect place for you to start. I just got a letter from the school asking for twenty dollars for graduation fees and saying you still owe thirty-two bucks for that history textbook you lost last year. Well, we're not paying for them. You are!"

That's when Ron walked in the door from work. "Paying for what?" he said.

Mom clearly didn't expect him home that soon. She handed me my jacket and said, "Oh, nothing," like we were just having a friendly little chat. Ron wasn't going to take that for an answer. He slammed his lunch box on the kitchen table.

She told him.

I knew it was going to be bad. He didn't say anything for a while. He just stared at me and took these long slow breaths.

"Sorry," I said. "I forgot."

He went nuts at that.

"Forgot? *Forgot*!" According to him, I'd forgotten everything they'd ever taught me. Manners. Common sense. Discipline. Respect for authority. Ambition. He went on and on.

All I could think was, "Yeah. Some fat-assed truck driver talking to me about ambition."

I couldn't take that kind of two-faced crap anymore. I picked up my jacket and started to walk out.

Ron pushed my mother aside and started coming after me. "You're not going anywhere, boy!"

"Yeah," I said. "So you tell me." I didn't even have to run. That slob couldn't catch me. I just walked out and slammed the door.

Chapter Four

It was still pissing rain. I walked around with my hood up and my hands in my pockets until I couldn't stand it. I found a Burger King and went in to warm up. I wasn't going to eat, but the fries smelled so good I couldn't help it. I ordered a combo. Lucky I still had the wallet with me.

By the time I finished eating, the rain had stopped. It was only about nine. I couldn't go home yet. My mother worked the early shift, so she'd be in bed, but Ron would still be up, cursing at the TV, just dying to get his hands on me. I didn't need him telling me what a loser I was again. I'd had enough of that for one day.

I guess I could have gone to Matt's, but he'd know something was up. I don't like talking to my friends about my life. His parents are normal. He wouldn't get it.

Somehow that made me mad again. This guy across from me tucked a napkin into his collar. I guess he didn't want his cheeseburger dripping on his fancy suit. Like we're all supposed to be impressed he wears a suit or something. I wanted to chuck my Coke at him so bad.

I had to get out before I did something stupid. I had to burn off some energy. I had to be too frigging tired to care by the time I got home. I needed to do something.

I didn't have a lot of options. I hate running, and it's not like I belong to a gym.

I decided to just return the wallet.

I checked the ID cards for an address. The guy lived at 27 Waterloo Crescent. It was a bit of a hike, but I didn't care. It was something to do.

It took me about half an hour to get there. Waterloo was in the good part of town, near the river. The houses were huge. They made our place look like a frigging garden shed.

Number 27 was a big brick house with a three-car garage and this giant tree out front. There wasn't a light on in the whole place. It looked like everyone was either gone or asleep. I walked up to the front door anyway. I'd come that far, why wouldn't I? I figured the guy would be glad to get his wallet back even if I woke him up. I rang the doorbell and waited.

No answer.

I rang it again. I tried to peek in through the curtains. For a fancy place, the room looked pretty bare. Just a leather couch and a big flat-screen TV. It could have used a carpet, but otherwise it looked okay to me. I didn't mind it so empty. Our living room was full of stuff, but everything was crap.

There was a mailbox on the wall beside the door. I thought about leaving the wallet there. I took it out of my pocket. The guy would find it the next day when he went to get his mail.

But what if he'd moved? Maybe that's why the place looked so deserted. Or what if he never got any mail? Or what if some crooked mailman took the wallet before the guy found it?

I thought of something else too. That old man. I'd told him there was seventy-five bucks in the wallet. He saw my face. What if, by some weird coincidence, he knew the guy who owned the wallet? What if he found out there was only sixty bucks left in it? He'd know I'd taken the money. It would be just my luck for something like that to happen. I'd be screwed.

There were lots of good reasons not to leave the wallet in the mailbox. I put it back in my pocket. I'd replace the money. I'd call the guy beforehand to make sure he was there. I'd come back another day.

Chapter Five

Ron was passed out in front of the TV when I got home. The guy was too lazy to even stay up and get mad at me. He was gone to work by the time I woke up the next morning.

My mother called in sick that day. She was waiting for me in the kitchen when I came down for breakfast. She tried to apologize. She said that money was tight.

That she was just upset. That she didn't mean that stuff about me being stupid.

Yeah, right. So why did she say it then?

I don't hate her. She's my mom. She's stuck with Ron—but still. I wasn't going to let her off that easy. I didn't say anything. I just shrugged. I grabbed my backpack and a cold English muffin and left. I had to get out of the house.

I made it to school fifteen minutes early. That was lucky. I'd forgotten to do my math homework. I'd kind of had other things on my mind that night.

Oxner would kick me out for sure if it wasn't done. Other teachers might cut me some slack if I told them about the "problems at home," but not him. I wouldn't give him the chance. There's no way I'd even tell him. I wasn't going to let him feel sorry for me.

I had to get some of the homework done or I was screwed.

I was leaning against my locker, staring at the math sheet, when I saw Alexa. One minute your life is total crap, and the next it seems like everything is one hundred percent okay.

"Hey, Alexa!" I said.

I didn't think she heard me. I ran after her.

"Alexa!"

That time she turned around. "Oh, hi, Christopher," she said. Her eyes were this amazing color, like a blue highlighter. I wondered if she wore tinted contacts.

"Can you do me a favor?" I said. Girls like her can't say no to a favor.

I explained that I'd had a little trouble getting my homework done the night before. I didn't tell her about my stepdad. It made me sound too much like trailer trash. I just asked if I could see her paper.

"Oh, I don't know about that, Christopher," she said. The way she looked, you'd think I was asking her to smuggle drugs into the country. "It's sort of cheating." She hugged her binder really close to her chest.

"Not for you it isn't," I said. "If anyone finds out, just tell the truth. Tell them I stole your binder." I yanked it out of her hands. She lost her balance. I caught her with my other arm just before she fell forward. It was pretty sweet.

"Please?" I whispered. "No one will know. I'll only copy enough answers so Oxner can't kick me out."

She stood up straight and smoothed her shirt. I could tell she didn't want to do it.

"Please," I said again.

She looked down the hall. It was like she was scared someone was watching.

"No one will find out," I said. I smiled at her. I have a nice smile. Girls always say that.

She bit her lower lip. She looked around again. She sighed.

"Okay," she said. "But hurry."

I messed up her hair and ran into the boys' washroom. It only took me about three minutes to get enough answers to keep Oxner off my back.

She was with some other girls when I came out. I put my arm around her so they wouldn't notice me slipping her the binder. When they left, I whispered, "Thanks. I'll make it up to you."

I'd have to think of something good.

Chapter Six

I ate my supper in my room that night. I felt kind of bad about leaving Mandy and Mom with Ron, but I couldn't hack the guy right then.

Besides, I needed to study too. It's one thing to get in trouble. Alexa didn't mind me giving Oxner a hard time. It's another thing looking stupid. I didn't want her thinking I was flunking out because I was dumb. I figured if I studied I could answer some questions in history the next day. That might impress her.

I opened the book. We were studying the Nazis. They were twisted enough that they were kind of interesting. I read for about half an hour, and then I started to think about Alexa again. Why wait until the next day? Why not call her now? I could act like I had some big question that just couldn't wait. I could make it sound like I actually spent time thinking about history and stuff like that.

I took her number out of the wallet. I was going to ask her when Hitler came to power. I punched in the first six numbers, and then I stopped. It was a dumb question. The answer was right there on the first page. If I asked her that, she'd think I couldn't read.

I hung up the phone. I looked at the book again. It said that Hitler was a vegetarian. I could ask Alexa if that's why she decided to give up meat. Say something like, "What? You trying to be just like Adolf? Is he your idol or something?" She might find that funny.

Then again, I thought, she might find it insulting. You never can tell with girls like her.

I read some more, but it didn't help. I couldn't think of a good question. They all made me sound like an idiot. I chucked the book across the room. Ron shouted, "What's going on up there?" and started swearing like I'd just kicked out the window. I put Alexa's number back in the wallet.

I lay on my bed and looked at the ceiling. I wanted to get out of the house, but I couldn't face walking past Ron right then. I was stuck in my room. There wasn't much I could do. I was sick of reading. I couldn't call Alexa. I couldn't even listen to music. My batteries were all dead.

Life sucked.

I told myself that some day I was going to live in one of those big houses on Waterloo Crescent. I'd have three cars in the driveway and a big lawn that somebody else would have to mow. I'd ask Ron over for supper just so I could see the look on his face when I told him how much I paid for the place.

I'd love that.

I took the wallet out. I had to see what type of person lived in a house like that.

The guy's name was Andrew Kirk Ashbury. His driver's license said he was twenty-five. I was all pissed off again. The guy was only eight years older than me and he already owned a big frigging mansion.

Or maybe he didn't, I thought. Maybe it was his parents' place.

That pissed me off too. I mean, he's in his twenties and still living with Mom and Dad! I was willing to bet little Andrew didn't have to work checkout at the grocery store. I figured he had it all just handed to him on a silver platter.

I looked at his driver's license. He was five foot nine, 150 pounds and had blue eyes. What do you know? Same as me. I almost laughed. Funny how we could be so much alike and so different at the same time. Andrew Ashbury got everything he could ever want and I got nothing.

How did that happen? How come I got stuck with the crap end of the stick?

I stared at his face. What was so great about him? He was no better than me. So he had short blond hair and I had long brown hair. So he wore glasses and I didn't. So he had an earring and I hated those things. He sure didn't look too special. The big man barely looked like he shaved, and I'd had a beard since I started high school.

I dumped everything out of the wallet onto my bed. I couldn't believe all the cards. I have a birth certificate and my last year's student card. (I was too broke to buy one this year.) Andrew had a driver's license, a birth certificate, four credit cards, a couple of gas cards and a bank card, not to mention a bunch of bonus cards for video stores, coffee shops, air miles, stuff like that.

I checked out his signature. It was this big, flashy bunch of loops with a line underneath. It was like he was just trying to see if his pen had any ink. You couldn't make out a single letter.

I really hated him when I saw that. Like, who did he think he was? Donald Trump?

I can't stand guys who act like they're too busy to write out their names.

I emptied the change pocket. He had two dollars and thirty-seven cents in coins, a key, a couple of business cards, a dry-cleaning receipt and a ticket for a baggage claim or something.

The only other thing in the wallet was a photo of this really hot girl. She had too much makeup on, but I could have lived with that. For the long red hair, I'd take all that eye shadow any day.

I flipped the picture over. It said, *For my boo. Love ya! JJ.* Her handwriting was really neat and perfect, like she taught kindergarten or something. (How come my teachers never looked like that?)

I looked at her for a while.

Frig.

Ashbury even got the girl! The house. The money. The girl. Everything. That pissed me off so much. I couldn't stand it. I felt like I was going to explode. Like some animal inside me was going to just bust out and start tearing the place apart.

I wanted to break something. I wanted to smash my fist through the wall, over and over again. The cheap frigging walls in this dump would crumble like potato chips. It would feel so good.

There was a place by the window that was already cracked and moldy from where the water leaked in. It would be perfect. I clenched my fist and pulled back my arm.

I stopped.

I remembered Ron, downstairs, just waiting for me to screw up again. I thought about Mandy and Mom and all the screaming if we got into it. I thought about Alexa.

I stared at the wall. I pounded my fist into my other hand. I had to do it over and over again, as hard as I could, but it worked. I didn't need to hit the wall anymore. I just looked at it. I imagined it crumbling. I pictured me busting out of the hole like this was a jailbreak or something.

That's what I needed to do. Escape. I knew I had to find another way to get out of this place.

I picked up all the cards and stuff and put them back in the wallet. I tried to put them in just the way they were before. I put Alexa's number in my back pocket. I counted the money left. About fifty-seven dollars. The next day I'd borrow eighteen dollars from my sister, and then I'd call Ashbury on the phone.

I figured a rich guy like him would probably give me a nice reward for returning his wallet safe and sound.

That would be my first step out of here.

Chapter Seven

I don't know why I'd been so worried about upsetting Mandy that night. I don't know why I even bothered trying to be nice to her. A lot of good it did me.

The next morning, I got up early. I knocked on her bedroom door. She went, "What?!" like she was already pissed off at me about something.

"Can I come in?" I said.

She went, "Why?"

"Because I want to ask you something." I said it nicely but it didn't make any difference.

"Forget it!" she said. She didn't even open the door. "I'm not lending you any money, Chris. You still owe me eleven dollars from last week!"

It really bugged me how she automatically assumed I was going to ask her for money, but I didn't let it show.

I tried to explain that I'd pay it all back in a couple of days. I'd even throw in a couple of bucks extra, but she just went, "Yeah, right. How dumb do you think I am? Like I haven't heard that before? Why don't you just get a job instead of bumming money off everyone? I babysit three days a week. I work for my money. You could too—if you weren't such a waste!"

"A waste." I was fine until she said that. She sounded just like Ron. She hated the guy—but it was me she was calling a waste.

I lost it. I kicked the door and swore at her. She screamed. Ron came running out of the bathroom with his fat gut hanging over the top of his pants and shaving cream all over his face. He started screaming too. Mom came running upstairs. She just went, "Chris!" She didn't even bother asking whose fault it was.

Everyone was screaming. No one was listening. What chance did I have?

They could all just screw themselves.

I grabbed my backpack and took off. Mom put her arm out to stop me as I went past. I knocked it away. She stumbled back down the stairs. I didn't care. For once, Ron looked like he was actually going to help her.

Good. Because I wasn't going to do it anymore.

I was out of there.

Chapter Eight

By the time I got to school I was feeling better. Better than I had in a long time. For once, I had a plan. I had some hope. I'd get the reward. I'd get out of there. I could go stay with my cousin out west. He'd put me up for a while. I could find a job. Get on my feet. Things were going to be okay.

Alexa walked into Oxner's class. She had on a pink shirt. The top two buttons were open. She sat down at the desk in front of me. I could smell her shampoo. She reached back and pulled her ponytail tight. Her fingers were really long and thin.

I wasn't sure I wanted to go after all.

If I dropped out of school, I'd never get a girl like Alexa. Sleeping on my cousin's couch, working at some crappy job—where would that get me? Not to some big mansion on Waterloo Crescent, that's for sure.

I had to think this through some more.

The PA came on and cut Oxner off. I'm never sorry when that happens. The principal announced that tickets for the school dance were only on sale until 3:00 PM that day. "Be there or be square," he said. The guy's pathetic.

I wasn't planning on going. I never went to school dances. I never had the money.

I had the money now, though. I'd just borrow some more from the wallet.

No, I wouldn't. I wouldn't borrow it. I'd *take* the money. I'd call Ashbury and tell him I found the wallet, but there was no cash in it. What would a guy like him care about seventy-five bucks? He'd be glad just to get his cards and stuff back. They were still worth a reward. I'd let drop that I lived on Fuller Terrace. He'd know anyone living in a place like that could use some money. Maybe he'd turn out to be a nice guy after all and give me something good.

For a second, I thought about the old man again. Why had I ever worried about him? What were the chances that he even knew Ashbury? What were the chances that he'd remember me? The guy was ancient. He probably couldn't even remember his own name.

I tapped Alexa on the shoulder. I whispered, "Hey! How'd you like to..."

She put her finger to her lips and went "Shhh!"

Oxner heard her. He turned around. He looked at me. "What's going on here?" he said and started coming down the aisle. He was just itching to haul me out of class.

Alexa said, "Sorry. That was me, Mr. Oxner. I thought I was going to sneeze."

Oxner looked at Alexa. He looked at me. He stood there, squinting, for a while, trying to figure out what to do, and then he just turned and walked back to the board. I touched Alexa on the shoulder and whispered thanks. She nodded but kept looking straight ahead for the rest of the class. She's the type that writes down everything the teacher says.

The bell rang. I was going to ask Alexa to the dance then, but Oxner wanted to talk to me. He said, "Don't think you can pull the wool over my eyes, Mr. Bent. I don't know what you were up to, but I know you were up to something."

He went on and on. I wasn't going to let myself get mad. I couldn't screw up now. I just had to think about something else and wait until he was finished.

I thought about going to the dance with Alexa. Ron would have a heart attack. Me going to the dance with his boss's daughter. He was going to love that.

Chapter Nine

I didn't see Alexa for the rest of the morning. No surprise. It's not like we hung out in the same crowds or anything. I'd ask her to the dance before history class.

I hadn't had any breakfast that day. I was starving. I headed to the cafeteria to see if I could bum some fries off someone. Then I realized I didn't have to. If I was going to tell Ashbury there was no money in the wallet when I found it, I could spend what was left. That meant I had enough to buy the tickets to the dance and get myself something to eat.

I decided to go to the Big Slice for pizza. I was thinking if I was lucky, Alexa might even be there. I left the schoolyard and was turning onto Windsor Street when I bumped into someone. I didn't even see him coming. Alexa did that to me.

We both said sorry at the same time. I looked up. It was the old man and his dog. He jumped back. His eyes went all big. He yanked the leash, and then he and his dog took off running.

It freaked me out, him running like that. The guy remembered me all right. He looked at me like I was some kind of criminal.

I didn't go to the Big Slice after all. I went back to school. I suddenly wanted to get rid of the wallet as fast as I could. I didn't even like having it on me.

I took the money from the wallet and put it in my pocket. Even if I got caught, no one would be able to tell it was

Ashbury's money. If anyone asked, I'd say I won it playing poker. Matt would back me up. Maybe sometime later I'd tell him the truth.

I went out behind the cafeteria. There was a Dumpster there I could chuck the wallet in. The truck would take the garbage away and no one would ever know I had it.

When I got there, a bunch of guys were hanging out behind the Dumpster, smoking. I couldn't very well throw the wallet away then. They'd want to know where I got it. They'd want to know why I was throwing it away. I hung around and bummed a smoke, as if that had been my plan all along.

By the time the bell rang, I'd calmed down. Maybe the cigarette helped or maybe it was the fact that I knew what the other guys there had gotten away with. This thing was nothing compared to some of the stuff they did. I'd been acting like a wuss. The old guy recognized me. So what? I'd scared him. There was no crime in that. He'd probably forgotten all about the wallet. It would be stupid to just throw it away and not even try to get a reward. I didn't want to end up the kind of guy that hangs out behind Dumpsters smoking someone else's cigarettes. I wanted to have some cash in my pocket when I took Alexa to the dance. We'd probably be hungry afterward. I said, "See ya," stubbed out my cigarette and went back inside.

I stopped at the office. The secretary didn't look too thrilled to see me. She raised her eyebrows when I bought two tickets to the dance. I guess she'd just figured I was there for some more "disciplinary" crap.

I saw Alexa walking down the hall to history. She was alone. It looked like a good opportunity. I ran up to her.

"Hey, Alexa!" I said. She turned around. She looked worried about something, but she smiled anyway.

"Oh, hi," she said. "We don't have any history homework due today."

I said, "Is that the only reason you think I talk to you?" and gave her a little nudge with my elbow.

"No, I guess not," she said. She went all blotchy again. She's the first person I'd ever met who actually blushed.

"Can you guess why I want to talk to you now?" I said.

She shook her head.

"I'll give you a hint—Friday night." I tilted my head and looked her right in the eye. "C'mon. Take a guess. You're a smart girl…"

She was really blushing now. It was obvious she knew what I was getting at, but she just shrugged.

"Okay, I'll tell you then," I said. "I got two tickets for the dance. One's for you—that is, if you want it…"

I smiled. I put my arm around her shoulders. I felt her neck go all tight. She stopped walking. She went, "Um, Christopher…"

I don't remember exactly what she said after that. Why bother even listening? It was all a load of crap. She could tell me how busy she was, how many commitments she had.

She could come up with any damn excuse she wanted. It didn't make any difference. In the second she turned and looked at me, I saw what she really meant.

It all boiled down to this: *Are you serious? Me? Alexa Doucette? Go out with a piece of garbage like you?*

I cut her off. I said, "Yeah, yeah. Whatever," and threw the tickets in her face. I called her a couple of names, and then I left. She wasn't blushing anymore. She was white as those fancy teeth of hers.

Chapter Ten

Oxner just happened to walk down the hall while I was kicking the crap out of my locker. He grabbed me by the jacket. I elbowed him in the gut. He called for help. I swore and took off. No use hanging around to hear what the principal had to say. I knew I was out of there for good.

I couldn't go home. I couldn't go to the Big Slice. I couldn't go to Matt's. (His mother would want me to "work my problems out" with the school, my parents, the whole frigging world. As if.) I couldn't go out west to stay with my cousin. You need more than forty-seven bucks to do that. I didn't know where to go.

I wondered if Oxner had called the cops. He was just the kind of wuss who'd be dialing 9-1-1 and screaming emergency because of a dented locker. I needed to disappear before they showed up. I didn't want them dragging me to jail or, even worse, home.

I saw a bus coming—the number 24. It was heading uptown. I got on. I needed a chance to figure things out. The bus was pretty empty, but I went right to the back anyway. I slouched down in the seat. I wanted to disappear.

For a while I didn't do anything. I just looked out the window. It was a nice day. Girls were already out in sleeveless shirts. I almost forgot about stuff.

The bus stopped at a park by the river. I wasn't planning on getting out, but I saw the river and I saw a phone booth. Something just hit me. I got off.

I knew I was near Waterloo Crescent. I'd phone Ashbury, give him the wallet and get the reward. I looked up his number in the book and dialed. The phone rang and rang. I was just about to give up when a woman answered.

She went, "Hello-o!" as if she was singing or something.

I said, "May I please speak with Andrew Ashbury?" When I was little, my mother made sure I knew how to talk on the phone. It's one of the few things she did right. No one has to know you live in a dump when you talk on the phone. If you sound good, you could be anybody.

"You got the wrong number," the woman said. She wasn't singing now.

"Is this 555-1254?" I said. "I'm looking for Andrew Ashbury at 27 Waterloo…"

She said, "He doesn't live here! I told you, wrong number!" and hung up in my frigging ear.

I hate rude people. I was just trying to help the guy! I'd had enough of this crap. I slammed the phone down.

Then I picked it up and slammed it down again. And again and again.

Screw you, lady.

I sat down in the shade under a tree. A bunch of boats sailed by on the river. It pissed me off. It really burned me that there are people out there with enough money to go sailing on a Thursday afternoon while the rest of the world is slaving away trying to earn a living.

I bought myself a hot dog from a guy with a cart. Then I bought myself a pop too, and some chips. If they could sail, I could get something to eat.

I went back and sat under the tree. I ate my lunch and thought about Ashbury. This was his neighborhood. I bet he'd been to this park before. He might even have sat under this exact same tree. He might have eaten a hot dog, bought from the exact same guy. He might have looked out at the exact same view.

He might have done all the exact same things I was doing right then—but I knew it would have been entirely different for him. He wouldn't be eating his hot dog wondering where he was going to find enough money for his next meal. He wouldn't be thinking about where he was going to stay that night. He'd just be enjoying the view, thinking about JJ and what the two of them had planned for the weekend.

A guy like that wouldn't give me a reward. He wouldn't care about his stupid wallet.

I chucked the rest of my hot dog at some ugly pigeon. It took off. Even a stupid pigeon could get away whenever it wanted. I was stuck in my frigging life. I had to just sit there and watch other people make money, get girls, have fun, be somebody.

It wasn't fair. It wasn't my fault my parents couldn't get their crappy lives together. It wasn't my fault my mother had to quit hairdressing school when I was born. It wasn't my fault my father took off. It wasn't my fault Ron was a jerk, we lived in a hole, school sucked. I didn't ask to be born. If I did, I sure wouldn't have asked to be born into that screwed-up family. This was their fault—but I was the one who had to live with the consequences.

Well, frig that. No more. I'd had enough.

I realized what I was going to do. I should have thought of it earlier. I opened the wallet. I looked at that picture of Ashbury again. I counted the money I had left.

I'd passed a drugstore on the way here. I was going back to find it.

Chapter Eleven

It's all about looks. That's how people decide what they think about you. You look poor, they think you're stupid. You look rich, you're the smartest guy around. You look like Chris Bent, your life is crap. You look like Andrew Ashbury, who knows? I was ready to find out.

I was only going to buy the blond hair dye, a razor and a pair of scissors, but I saw some cheap reading glasses up by the counter. The brown ones were kind of like what Ashbury was wearing on his driver's license. I bought those too. Glasses make you look intelligent. The saleslady told me how to get to the public washroom.

I cut my hair. It was pretty much a hack job. Once I found work, I'd go to a barber and get it done right. I shaved off my beard. The razor was toast by the time I was done.

It felt weird. I'd had a goatee before, and a mustache, and even just a soul patch for a while, but I hadn't been clean-shaven since I was a kid. My skin felt really sensitive, as if I'd just taken off a wet shirt on a cold day. I liked it.

I'd watched my mother dye her hair for years. It wasn't that hard. I took off my T-shirt, put on the plastic gloves and squished the stuff all over my head. I rubbed some into my eyebrows too. Mine were too dark for someone blond.

I didn't want anyone to see what I was up to. I sat in a cubicle and waited for the dye to work. It was pretty boring. After a while, I took the wallet out again. If I was going to start applying for jobs, I needed to find out everything I could about Andrew Ashbury.

I already knew his address and his size. I memorized his birthdate and his postal code. I took a pen out of my backpack and practiced his signature, just in case I needed it. Four loops and a line. It was almost too easy.

What else did I need to do? I figured I should know something about his family, what he did for a living, stuff like that.

I looked all through the wallet again. There was nothing about his family. It didn't matter. If anyone asked, I'd just make something up. Joanna and Blake, those would be his parents. He'd have one brother, Bryce, and a sister, Ann-Marie. No, Marina. Bryce and Marina. When I'm rich, that's what I'm going to name my kids.

I thought about giving myself a dog too, but what I really wanted was a Doberman. Andrew wasn't the type to have a Doberman, and I didn't want some wussy little rich-kid dog. JJ probably had a cat. I could talk about her cat, how it bugs me, sheds on my clothes, hisses when I kiss her. Guys never like their girlfriends' cats.

I needed a hobby too. I thought of sailing, but I didn't know anything about boats. That was okay. I knew everything about cars, and now I was rich enough to own a couple too.

That stopped me. Who was I kidding? I wasn't rich enough to own anything yet. I had about three bucks in my pocket—but nobody needed to know that. Someday it would be different. I'd laugh about this.

I kept looking through the wallet. The business cards, baggage claim, key—they wouldn't help me. The dry-cleaning receipt, though, was for a suit and a shirt. It was marked "Paid." I checked the address. The dry cleaners wasn't far from here. Things were looking up. Maybe I could get rid of this old jacket.

I checked my watch. Fifteen minutes had passed. It was time to wash the stuff

out of my hair. I put the cards back in the
wallet. The ATM card was flipped over. I
picked it up and noticed something scratched
on the back. I moved it around in the light to
see if I could make it out: 2-5-3-7-9.

Or was that an eight?

As in 2-5-8-7-9. It was one or the other.

I couldn't believe it. Was this guy really
stupid enough to write his PIN number on the
back of his bank card? Nothing like this had
ever happened to me before. I saw a whole
bunch of new possibilities open up.

My heart was pounding so hard I could
feel it in my teeth.

I had to pull myself together. I couldn't
screw up now. I stuffed everything back in
the wallet. I needed to wash the dye out right
away. I sure wouldn't look like Ashbury if I
went bald.

I tucked the wallet into the front of my
pants, where it was safe. It was like a winning
lottery ticket now. I couldn't lose it. I bent over
the sink and washed my hair. I had to use that
gross pink hand soap from the dispenser. It
stunk, but it worked.

I.D.

I used a ton of paper towels to dry my
hair and a ton more to clean the place up.
I shoved them all into the garbage can. I
didn't need anyone wondering what had
gone on in here.

I took out Ashbury's driver's license. I
looked in the mirror. It was pretty close.
My nose was a bit bigger than his. I needed
an earring. I had a zit on my chin. He
didn't. I put on the glasses. I looked at the
picture again. I looked at me again.

Or was it me?

It was kind of hard to tell.

Chapter Twelve

The lady at the dry cleaners didn't even blink. I handed her the receipt and she just handed me back the suit and shirt.

"Have a nice day," she said.

I looked at the suit and went, "Yeah, you bet!"

Nice day? Nice life, more like it. I'd never had a suit before. No one in my family had one. Ron had to borrow a jacket from the guy next door for my grandmother's funeral. It didn't help. He still looked like a piece of garbage.

Not me though. I wouldn't. A black suit. A blue shirt. That would suit me fine. I'd look good in it. Successful. No one would think I had bummed it off a neighbor.

That suit was my ticket out of there. No more crappy jobs for me. With a suit like that on, I could go for a sales position. I had Ashbury's ID. With the glasses, I could pass for twenty-five. I could maybe even sell cars.

That would be right up my alley. I'd make lots of money. I'd buy myself lots of suits. Get myself lots of girls. Someday I'd come back here and call Alexa up, just to say hello. There was no way I'd ever ask her out again though. She'd missed her chance. I'd love to see her face when she figured that out.

I felt good. It was all going to happen. I just needed to get some cash, get this thing started.

There was an ATM in the mall. I waited until there was nobody around, and then I tried it. I checked the number on the back of the bank card. I was pretty sure it was 2-5-3-7-9.

I inserted the card, punched in the number and waited. It took a long time. Or at least it seemed like a long time. Everything seems to take a long time when you're scared.

And—I admit it—I was scared.

As soon as I keyed in the PIN, I realized that I didn't know what happened with stolen cards. What if Ashbury had reported it missing? Would an alarm go off? Was there a camera taking my picture right then? Would I be on *Crime Stoppers* that night?

The ATM beeped. I jumped as if I'd just got tasered or something. The screen read "Incorrect PIN. Cancel or try again?"

I could barely breathe. I didn't know what to do. It was like my whole life depended on which button I chose.

I could hit cancel and leave. That would be the safest thing. I could just forget about the cash, throw the wallet away like I had planned to.

But then what would I do? Where would I go? Not home. Not school. Not anywhere I knew, that's for sure.

I could hide my suit somewhere and live on the streets until I found a real job. I could just lie when I filled out applications and put down my grandmother's address. In the meantime I'd need some money though. I knew some squeegee kids who did okay. They always had more cash to throw around at the Big Slice than I ever did. I could do that for a while until something better came along. It didn't seem like a bad idea. I was a good cleaner. I liked cars. And it would be nice to have some money in my pocket. You get more respect with money in your pocket.

I suddenly had this image of myself. I'm at the stoplights. A BMW pulls up. I squeegee the windshield. I look inside. Alexa's driving. She tosses me some change and says, "Sorry, Christopher, that's all I've got right now." I don't believe her but I still scramble to catch whatever I can. That's how desperate I am.

No way.

I couldn't do it. I'm no squeegee kid. I've got more self-respect than that.

I couldn't stop now. I needed to make something out of my life. The bank card was my only hope.

What difference did it make anyway? It was too late to turn back now. If there was a camera on the ATM, it would have already taken my picture.

I just had to go for it.

I punched in 2-5-8-7-9.

The ATM beeped right away. The screen said *Deposit? Withdrawal? Account Balance?*

I started shaking. I was happy. I was proud. I was doing it. I was taking charge of my life.

I hit "Withdrawal." Then I hit "Checking." How much did I need?

I should have phoned around first. I should have found out how much a bus out west would cost. It would take a couple of days at least to get there. I'd need some money for food on the way. If my cousin couldn't pick me up at the station, I'd need to pay for a taxi. I'd need some cash when I got there too. Brandon could probably lend me a razor until I got a job, but I couldn't ask for more than that. I couldn't let him get pissed off at me. I didn't want him kicking me out too.

Two hundred dollars? Two hundred and fifty dollars? It sounded like a lot of money—but it didn't sound like enough either. Maybe I should just take two hundred dollars now and get another two hundred dollars later. I didn't want to withdraw too much at once. The bank might get suspicious.

Then again, I thought, this could be my last chance. Ashbury might just be getting around to reporting his wallet missing. The next day the card might not work. The next day I might have lost my nerve.

I split the difference. I punched in three hundred dollars. I worried there might not be that much in the account, but then I heard the ATM doling out the money. Two seconds later, it spit out a big wad of cash and a receipt.

The twenty-dollar bills were all warm and smooth, as if they were just fresh from the laundry. I couldn't help myself. I flicked the end of the wad with my thumb as if I were shuffling cards. I had to bite my lips to keep from grinning like an idiot.

I pulled myself together. I didn't have time for this. I couldn't hang around and have someone notice me. I needed to get out of there. I put the card and the cash in the wallet, just like any normal person would. Like it was no big deal. I glanced at the receipt and threw it in the garbage.

I picked up my suit and my backpack and turned to go. Then I stopped. The number I read on the receipt flashed in my mind. Could it be right?

I ran back and pulled the receipt out of the wastepaper basket. I looked at it again. I had to say the number out loud, just so it made sense.

"Account balance: $67,482.72."

Chapter Thirteen

The suit fit perfectly. It looked great with the blue shirt. I didn't have a tie, but I didn't care. Lots of guys wear suits without ties nowadays. It looks more casual that way.

My old brown shoes would have to go though. I mean, there's casual and then there's crap. They were crap. They made the suit look bad.

There was a shoe store in the mall. I'd get something there. I stuffed my old clothes and my backpack into the garbage can. I wouldn't be needing them anymore. I was lucky. I left the washroom without anyone seeing me go in or out.

A black shoe made the most sense. It would go with anything. The sales guy brought me a few to try on. I liked the loafers best. I shoved my old shoes under the bench and put the loafers on. I was going to wear them out of the store.

I said, "I'll take them." I didn't even ask what they cost.

He said, "That will be ninety-two dollars and sixty-four cents, sir. How will you be paying for that?"

I understood what he meant, but for a second I thought he was saying, "How the hell would someone like you have ninety-three bucks to spend on shoes?" It pissed me off. My head jerked up. I almost said something, but then I saw him smiling at me. He wasn't worried about me having enough money. I could tell he thought the suit was pretty sharp.

I went, "I don't know. Cash, I guess." I pulled out the wallet. It was so fat. I snapped the five twenties onto the counter, one by one. I said, "Just want to make sure no bills got stuck together." The sales guy told me some story about losing a fifty that way, and then he gave me my change. I stuffed the five-dollar bill in the little donation box they had for the children's hospital. There was no way a guy like that would be carrying two fifties around. I smiled at him anyway and left.

It must have been after six. I was starving. I was close to the food court. I could smell it. I smiled. Everything was so easy now. If I wanted something, I just got it. I was hungry, so I was going to eat.

The food court was crowded. I stood in line at the Barbecue Pit. I'd just about decided on the half chicken with the spicy dipping sauce when I changed my mind. I didn't want to get grease on my new suit. I could always buy another one of course. I *would* buy another one—but I still didn't want to be walking around until then with a big stain down my front.

I needed something dry and neat. A sandwich would be fine.

I pushed my way out of the Barbecue Pit lineup and headed over to Bagel Schmagel. There were all sorts of people coming at me with trays full of greasy food. I had to swerve to avoid them. The glasses I was wearing were a little too strong for me, I guess. I had trouble judging how far away things were. I banged my hip against a guy's table. Everything shook. I grabbed his coffee before it fell onto his plate of Chinese food.

I went, "Sorry," and handed the coffee back to him. The guy looked up. It was Oxner. Just my luck. Him, of all people. What was *he* doing here? I couldn't believe he ever even left the school.

I must have gone white. He looked right at me. I was just waiting for him to go, "Christopher Bent? Someone call the police!" But he didn't. He just soaked up the coffee with his napkin and said, "That's okay. No harm done." He gave me this lame smile.

"Right," I said and kept going.

I took a shortcut through the tables to the exit. Suddenly I felt surrounded by people I knew. People who knew *me*. I noticed Adriane Salah from my biology class talking with a bunch of girls by the Eatsa Pizza. A guy who looked kind of familiar was shoving down a burrito. A girl with big silver earrings was staring right at me.

I had to get out of there.

I didn't run, but I wanted to.

Chapter Fourteen

I got into the first cab I could find.

"Where to?" the driver said.

I wanted to say, "Just get me out of here," but that would look bad. He'd think something was up.

My mind went blank. I couldn't think of anywhere to go.

I went, "Ah…" The driver tapped on the steering wheel for a while. Then he flicked on the meter.

I had to be cool.

I said, "Know any nice hotels near the airport?" That sounded good to me. Sort of natural. The type of thing a businessman would say. The driver would just think I was someone passing through. He wouldn't take much notice of me. That's the way I wanted it.

"Yeah, sure," he said. "Sit back and relax. I'll have you there in a jiffy." He pulled out of the parking lot like he was driving a getaway car.

The highway gave me time to think. That thing in the food court was too close for comfort. How many people had seen me? How many people knew who I was? Maybe I was fooling myself. Maybe everyone could tell that blond guy was just Chris Bent in a suit and glasses.

I thought about Oxner. He had a weird look on his face. What was he thinking? Did he know it was me?

My heart went crazy for a while, and then it hit me. Oxner never missed a chance to get me in trouble. He'd probably spent that whole day plotting what he'd do when he finally got his hands on me. If he'd recognized me, he would have said something. I was sure of it.

But why the look on his face then?

Maybe Oxner just didn't like having some stranger's hand all over his coffee cup. It would sure gross me out—even if the guy was wearing a nice suit.

Then I remembered that skuzzy mug Oxner kept on his desk. If he could drink out of that, he could drink out of anything. There was no way he would have cared about my hand on his coffee cup.

I pictured him again in the food court, looking up at me. He didn't look disgusted. His lip wasn't curled up or anything. He seemed more embarrassed, like he didn't want to have to talk to anyone, like he just wanted to go back to being by himself.

That was it.

Oxner was embarrassed! I knew why too. He was embarrassed by his sad little life. He got caught all alone, eating some plate of greasy sweet-and-sour pork in some pathetic food court. He gets to act like some big shot at school all day, but the truth is he's nothing. You can tell just by those stupid polo shirts he wears. The guy probably lives in some stinking little basement apartment. He's got no wife, no friends, no life. He goes to the mall to get away from it all. Then some young guy in an expensive suit bangs into his table and reminds him what a failure he is.

It made sense. That's why he looked so weird. He was humiliated. Suddenly, I couldn't have been happier.

I relaxed. I watched the trucks whiz by. I wasn't so worried about those other people in the food court anymore either. Adriane Salah probably didn't even see me. She was too busy laughing with her friends. The guy eating the burrito looked familiar but so what? Guys in their forties basically all look the same. The girl with the big earrings was staring at me all right, but I could explain that too. Girls look at guys. She was probably wondering who I was. I bet if I'd hung around a while longer she would have come up with some excuse to talk to me.

The driver pulled up in front of the Aerolux Inn. "That will be twenty-six dollars and twenty-five cents, sir."

That kind of shocked me. I didn't think it would be that much. I knew it didn't matter. I had the money in my wallet. I had tons in my bank account, but still. It was going so fast. What if I couldn't get to an ATM before I ran out of cash? What if Ashbury reported his card missing?

What if Oxner did recognize me after all?

I was getting nervous again.

The cabdriver didn't look so pleasant anymore. I guess he didn't like the way I wasn't paying him.

I couldn't spend any more money.

"Do you take Visa?" I said.

The guy wasn't happy about it, but he took it. I gave him a ten-dollar tip and signed the slip. Four loops and a line.

The guy tore off a copy of the receipt and handed it back to me. "Thanks, Mr. Ashbury," he said. "Enjoy your stay."

Chapter Fifteen

I could feel sweat trickling down my back, my ribs, my stomach. I was going to ruin my suit. There'd be salt stains all over it.

I was such an idiot! Why did I go and use the Visa? Now the cabdriver knew my name! What if there was a thing in the paper about the missing wallet? What if the cabdriver called the police?

There was a guy in a uniform standing by the door of the hotel. "Are you all right, sir?" he said.

"Yeah, yeah, I'm fine," I said. "Just a little warm. Any place I could get a drink around here?"

"We have a very nice bar just beyond the front desk, sir," he said. He held the door open for me. The blast of air-conditioning felt good. I went to the bar.

It was a classy place. Dark wood. Big armchairs. My grandmother would have liked the music they piped in. I sat at a table in the corner. The waitress came over pretty fast. I guess there wasn't much else for her to do. The place was practically deserted.

She put a napkin and a little bowl of peanuts on the table. She was pretty. I bet she was only about twenty-one.

"What can I get you, sir?" she said.

I probably should have ordered a martini or a scotch in a place like that, but I'm not big on hard liquor. That stuff makes you crazy. I saw what it did to my stepdad. I ordered a beer. She didn't even ask for ID. That calmed me down a bit.

She brought the beer. I wanted it so bad, but I made myself pour it into the glass first.

"Will you be keeping a tab, sir?" she said. I nodded. I didn't know if I'd want another beer or not, but I couldn't pay right then. I was too freaked out. I couldn't touch the wallet. I didn't even like thinking about it. I needed time.

I downed half of the beer in one gulp. I waited for it to kick in. I ate some peanuts. I leaned back in the chair. I listened to the music. I was starting to feel better. I could think straight again.

Things weren't that bad. The guy lost a wallet with seventy-five bucks in it. Big deal. He's not going to be calling the police about that! The cabdriver would have no reason to know the name Andrew Ashbury. He'd have no reason to remember me. He probably drove twenty people a day to the airport. A young guy in a suit. Why would he remember me?

I was being a wuss. I was getting hysterical, like some old lady. I didn't need to worry—about that anyway.

I finished the beer. I called the waitress over. I ordered another. I asked her if there was an ATM around here.

"There's one in the lobby, sir," she said.

My plan was changing. I went to the bank machine. There were taxis waiting out front. I punched in a five hundred-dollar withdrawal. If the card was declined, I'd just jump in one of the cabs and take off. I hoped the waitress wouldn't be stuck paying my tab. I'd probably just go to the bus station from there.

Turns out I didn't have to worry. I got the five hundred dollars, no problem. I stuffed it in the side pocket of my wallet, away from the other money. It was my nest egg. I couldn't touch it.

My beer was waiting for me when I got back. I called the waitress over again and ordered a steak. This would be my last good meal for a while. I figured I might as well enjoy it.

The steak was perfect—about two inches thick, with those black crisscross lines all over it like you see in the commercials. I could have cut it with a butter knife. It was a whole lot better than that crap Oxner was eating.

I kind of laughed when I thought about all that bright pink sauce on Oxner's sweet-and-sour pork. I guess he wasn't worried about staining his "windbreaker."

Then I had another thought. It wasn't just a coincidence that I bumped into Oxner in the mall. That was just too weird. I suddenly knew there was a reason for it.

I was being given a warning. A reminder to be careful. I didn't know by who. God? The universe? Or maybe it was my grandmother, reaching out to me from, you know, "beyond the grave."

You hear about that stuff all the time on television. A bird lands on someone's shoulder at the exact second his brother dies a million miles away. A person sees a light in the woods and gets out of the car just before the engine explodes. A woman hears a piano playing in an empty house and finds a diamond ring hidden under the lid. Those can't just be coincidences. Some dead person is communicating with them. Just because you can't prove it doesn't mean it's not true.

Nan and I were close. She was always there for me. I figured this was her way of telling me to watch out. My luck wasn't going to last forever.

And anyway, she'd be the first person to tell me not to depend on luck. She'd tell me I needed to do this myself. I needed to take charge of my life.

I took the last bite of steak. Nan was right.

My marks sucked, but I was smart. Smarter than Oxner, that's for sure. I could do this. I didn't need to take somebody else's money. I just needed a loan until I could get myself started. Someday, I'd track Andrew Ashbury down. I'd invite him to a nice restaurant like this and tell him the whole story. I'd pay him back everything, plus interest. Just to make up for it, I'd invite him for a sail on my private yacht. We might even become friends.

For now, though, I needed to get out west where nobody knew me. That's what Nan was trying to tell me. My cousin could be trusted. I had the suit to help me get a job. I had the money to help Brandon out with the rent until my first paycheck came through.

The waitress came over. "How was everything, sir?"

"Fine," I said. "There was just one problem."

She frowned. She was still pretty.

"What's that, sir?"

"I don't like you calling me sir," I said. "I get enough of that all day." I winked at her. She laughed.

I knew it wouldn't be long before I could say that for real. Maybe, when I came back, I'd ask her out.

Chapter Sixteen

I couldn't take a bus out west. I had to get away faster than that. And anyway, two days on a bus would ruin my suit. I'd have to fly.

I took the shuttle to the airport. It was a free service. I'd never been on a plane before. I'd never even been in an airport. I thought I'd be nervous, but I was okay. The place looked just like airports always do in the movies.

I went up to the ticket counter. I asked when the next flight to Edmonton was. The lady punched a bunch of things into the computer.

She said, "The seven-forty flight is full, but we have a couple of seats on the ten-thirty flight."

That was fine with me. She typed in some other stuff. It took her forever. She asked for my ID. I didn't even have time to panic. I just handed her my driver's license. She didn't bat an eye. She seemed more surprised that I didn't have any luggage.

"Okay," she said. "That will be $987. 46."

I couldn't help myself. I went, "What?! A thousand bucks?"

"Last-minute tickets are always more expensive, sir. If you'd prefer to fly stand-by I could get you a cheaper fare, but I can't guarantee you'll get on the flight." She smiled. You could tell she couldn't care less how much this was costing me.

I should have taken more money out. I didn't want to go to an ATM now. I'd look like some hick who didn't keep enough cash on him. I could ask if they'd take debit. But what if they didn't? I'd look like someone who'd never flown before.

"Fine," I said. "I better take it. I've got a meeting I can't miss."

I handed her the Visa card. She swiped it. I concentrated on breathing, looking relaxed. I tried not to think about all the cops I'd seen hanging around the airport in their bulletproof vests.

The machine buzzed. The receipt came out. She ripped it off. I signed it. She handed me my boarding pass and told me to be at Gate 23 by 9:50. She reminded me to have picture ID to show the flight attendants.

I went to the washroom. I thought I was going to puke. This was like playing Russian roulette. How many blanks could I fire before I got hit by a real bullet? I couldn't stand it anymore. If I didn't need ID to get on the plane, I would have thrown the wallet away right then.

I splashed cold water on my face and tried to calm down. I looked in the mirror. My haircut looked like crap. Ashbury would never have a bad haircut. He could afford a good one. It was going to look suspicious.

No, I couldn't think that way. I was okay. No one was going to notice my haircut. The Visa went through, no problem. Ashbury obviously hadn't reported anything missing yet.

But why? It had been three days since I found that wallet. Why wouldn't he have reported it? He might not have cared about the seventy-five bucks, but no one wants their Visa floating around on the street. Someone could find it, rack up a whole bunch of charges.

I wondered if Ashbury was away somewhere and hadn't noticed his wallet was gone. Or maybe he was sick in bed and didn't need it.

Or maybe he was dead.

That gave me goose bumps. Looking in the mirror, seeing Ashbury's face, thinking he was dead.

It dawned on me that maybe this was like reincarnation. Maybe Ashbury really was dead. Maybe I was meant to take over his identity. Maybe no one would ever know the difference. Chris Bent would just disappear and be replaced by a new Andrew Ashbury.

That was too weird to even think about. I got the creeps. I dried myself off and left the washroom.

I had three hours to kill. I decided to call Brandon and tell him I was coming. I found a phone, but then I realized I couldn't call him collect. He'd never accept the call. I had some money but I didn't want to spend it. I had to be careful. I didn't know when I'd get more. I could have used the Visa, but that was starting to make me too nervous. I didn't know what my limit was. From now on, I was only going to use it for emergencies.

I decided I'd just call Brandon when I got there. It would be a local call. It wouldn't cost much. That was better anyway. If I called him from Edmonton, he couldn't turn me away. He'd have to let me stay.

I was going to call my mother and tell her I was leaving. Part of me didn't want her to worry. Another part, though, thought it served her right.

In the end, I didn't call. Ron might have picked up. I'd buy Mom and Mandy something nice as soon as I got a job. I'd mail it home with a letter. Someday I'd buy them tickets to come out and see me. Mom always wanted to visit Edmonton.

I wandered around the airport. There were lots of stores. I looked around for a while but then it got boring. Why go to a store if you can't spend any money?

I started to feel tired. I just wanted to sleep, wake up somewhere else. I found a place to sit down. Some people were passed out on the benches. They looked like bums. There was no way I'd do that. It didn't matter how tired I was.

I couldn't get comfortable. I was worried my jacket was going to get wrinkled. I would have taken it off, but I could feel my shirt was still sweaty. That would have looked gross. I really wished I had something else to put on. I needed to save my suit for job interviews.

That made me think of something. I
wasn't sleepy anymore. That slip of paper
Ashbury had in the wallet. Wasn't it for
luggage?

No one was looking. I opened the wallet
and took it out.

I remembered right. It was a baggage
claim for the airport. This airport. I read
it. It didn't say much. *No: 3904. One duffel
bag. To be held until May 23. ID must be
shown to collect all articles of luggage.*
There was some other stuff about what you
could leave there and what you couldn't,
but that didn't mean much to me.

I folded the paper back up and put it in
my pocket.

A duffel bag. Ashbury probably kept
his casual clothes in it. Jeans, T-shirts, that
kind of thing. Stuff he didn't mind getting
wrinkled. Stuff that would be comfortable
to wear on a plane. That's probably why he
left it there.

There was a little key in the wallet too.
I bet it was for the duffel bag. He didn't
want anyone stealing anything.

It was May 22. I knew that for sure because the dance was on the twenty-third. I thought of Alexa for a second. I realized I didn't care who she went to the dance with. That had nothing to do with my life.

This was my life now. There was still time. I could get out of this wet shirt. I could keep my suit looking nice.

It was just too perfect. I felt like my grandmother was smiling down on me again. I wondered if she'd arranged this somehow too. Nan always made sure she looked good even if she didn't have much money.

I found a sign with a map of the airport. The baggage claims office was on the main floor. I had plenty of time before I had to be at the gate.

I was fine until I got to the escalator. More than fine. I was happy. Then, out of the blue, I started getting nervous again. I kept thinking, "ID must be shown." That zit on my chin was really big now. I guess it was nerves. Ashbury didn't look like the type to get acne. What twenty-five-year-old even gets pimples? A cop was coming up the escalator as I was going down. He looked right at me when we passed. I was sweating again, bad.

I almost turned around. Then I realized how stupid I was being. The lady who sold me the ticket had looked at my ID. Think how careful she had to be! She had to make sure she didn't let terrorists or criminals on the plane. She really looked at the picture on my license—and she didn't notice anything. She still sold me my ticket. This time, I was only going to pick up a duffel bag. Who was going to care about ID for something like that?

The office was easy to find. There was a bit of a lineup but that was okay. I had lots of time, and anyway, the guy at the counter was moving people through pretty fast. He sure wasn't studying anyone's ID to see whether the guy in the picture had a zit on his chin or not.

I was being a jerk. Zits come and go anyway.

Then I remembered the earring. Why didn't I get my ear pierced like Ashbury's?

There were plenty of places that would have done it in the mall. It would only have cost me about five bucks! It seemed like such a stupid way to get caught.

I couldn't think about that right then. There was nothing I could do about it.

There was only one more person ahead of me. The baggage claims guy was joking with her. That made me relax a bit. The guy didn't look like he was too hard-ass. If he noticed I didn't have an earring, I'd just say I wasn't wearing it that day.

How come I didn't have a hole in my ear then?

This was stupid. I had to be disciplined, act natural. The woman took her red suitcase and left.

"Next!" the guy said. "Yes, that would be you, sir. May I see your baggage claim?"

I handed it to him. He looked at it.

"Well, you got here just in the nick of time." He keyed the number of my claim into the computer.

"Hmm," he said. "I wonder why this is taking so long." I felt like puking again.

He stared at the screen for a while, typed a few more things in.

"I'm going to need to see your ID, Mr. Ashbury."

I took out my driver's license. The guy looked at it, looked at me and nodded.

"Yup. That's you all right."

I had to relax. I couldn't take this roller coaster anymore. The guy knew it was me. I was okay. It was just a duffel bag.

The guy said, "Wait right there. I'll be back in one sec."

It wasn't one sec. The guy was gone for like five minutes. He came out carrying a small brown duffel bag. It looked heavy. I hoped I could take it on the plane.

"Is this yours?" he said.

"It looks like mine," I said. It had a little lock on the zipper. I was pretty sure the key would open it.

He handed me the bag. I said, "Thanks," and turned around to leave.

The cop I'd seen on the escalator was right in front of me. He was pointing his gun at my head.

He didn't need to say anything. I was pretty sure I knew what had happened. I'd been waiting for it all along. Ashbury must have reported his cards missing. The bank must have got my picture from that ATM. The cabdriver and the lady at the ticket counter must have called me in too. I figured they all knew I wasn't Andrew Ashbury. I bet even the waitress knew it. I was just some kid from the crap side of town trying to act like the big man. They must have all been laughing their asses off.

But I was wrong.

Chapter Seventeen

The cop went, "Andrew Kirk Ashbury. You are under arrest for two counts of murder, forcible confinement, procurement of drugs for the purpose of trafficking, and possession of a firearm. You have the right to counsel. If you cannot afford counsel, it will be..."

I didn't understand him. He called me Andrew Kirk Ashbury. It didn't make sense. Two other cops had me cuffed and on my knees before it sank in.

I tried to tell them that I was Christopher Earl Bent. That I just found the wallet on the street. That they had the wrong guy. That I didn't know anything about murder or drugs or firearms.

But they just said, "Yeah, sure," and threw me in the back of their cruiser.

I looked out the back window. I could still see the airport.

I couldn't help it. I smiled. I'd almost made it.

Vicki Grant is the author of another Orca Soundings novel, *Dead-End Job*, and the recently released *Pigboy*, an Orca Currents novel. Her comic legal thriller, *Quid Pro Quo*, won the Arthur Ellis Award for Best Juvenile Crime Fiction and was shortlisted for the Edgar Allan Poe Award. Vicki lives in Halifax, Nova Scotia.

Titles in the
Orca Soundings series

Titles in the
Orca Soundings series

Titles in the
Orca Soundings series

Titles in the
Orca Soundings series

Tough Trails

Irene Morck

The Darwin Expedition

Diane Tullson

The Trouble with Liberty

Kristin Butcher

Truth

Tanya Lloyd Kyi

Wave Warrior

Lesley Choyce

Who Owns Kelly Paddik?

Beth Goobie

Yellow Line

Sylvia Olsen

Zee's Way

Kristin Butcher

Visit www.orcabook.com for more information.

Titles in the Orca Currents series